THIS WALKER BOOK BELONGS TO:

_____

_____

_____

_____

For Emily and Anna

Eating Out and *The Drive* first published 1983
Gran and Grandpa first published 1984
by Walker Books Ltd
87 Vauxhall Walk
London SE11 5HJ

This edition published 1995

2 4 6 8 10 9 7 5 3 1

© 1983, 1984 Helen Oxenbury

This book has been typeset in Goudy.

Printed in Hong Kong

British Library Cataloguing in Publication Data
A catalogue record for this book is available from the British Library.

ISBN 0-7445-3779-7 (hb)
ISBN 0-7445-3724-X (pb)

A Really Great Time

Gran and Grandpa 7

Eating Out 19

The Drive 33

Helen Oxenbury

WALKER BOOKS

AND SUBSIDIARIES

LONDON · BOSTON · SYDNEY

Gran and Grandpa

I love visiting my gran
and grandpa.
I go every week.

"Tell us what you've been doing
all week," they say.
I tell them everything.
Then sometimes I teach them
a new song I learnt at school.
But they never get the tune quite right.

"Come on, Gran!
Let's go and look at all
your things," I say.
Gran has such
interesting drawers
and boxes.

"How are your
tomatoes, Grandpa?"
"I've saved you the first
ripe one to pick,"
he says.

"Come and make a house
with me, Grandpa,"
I say.

"Lunch is ready!" calls Gran.
Grandpa can't get up.
"You shouldn't play these games
at your age," Gran tells him.

"We could play hospitals now,"
I say after lunch.

Gran and Grandpa let me do
anything to them.
"I'll just get more bandages," I say.
When I get back they're both asleep.
So I watch television quietly until
Dad comes.

Eating Out

Mum said, "I'm too tired
to cook."
Dad said, "I'll take you
out to supper."

"I suppose you need a high
chair," the waiter said.
The room was hot and stuffy.
We had to wait ages for the food.

"Why can't you sit still like those nice little children?" Dad said.

"Get back on your chair," Mum said. "Here comes your lovely meal."

25

"Why didn't you say you
wanted to go before the
food arrived?" Mum said.

I wasn't very hungry,
so I went under the table.
Someone trod on my foot.

The waiter made a terrible mess.
"That's that," Dad said.
"Never again," said Mum.
"Anyway, I like eating at
home the best," I said.

The Drive

One day we went for a drive.
Mum made some sandwiches.

"How can Daddy drive
properly with all that noise
going on?" Mum said.

I went with Dad
to pay for the petrol.
"Can't I just have some
little sweets?" I said.

At lunchtime we
went to a café.
I only wanted
ice-cream.

"Just have a little sleep now," Mum
said. "We won't be home till late."
"I want to go to the lavatory," I said.

"I think it's going to rain,"
  Mum said.
"My tummy hurts, I feel sick,"
  I said.
"Quick! Stop!" Mum shouted.

We cleaned up the
car. Then it wouldn't
start again. Dad tried,
but it was no good.
"I'll have to call a
garage for help," he said.

The truck towed us home.

"We've just had a really great time,"
I told my friends.

45

MORE WALKER PAPERBACKS
For You to Enjoy

Growing up with Helen Oxenbury

TOM AND PIPPO

There are six stories in each of these two colourful books about
toddler Tom and his special friend Pippo, a soft-toy monkey.

"Just right for small children… A most welcome addition to the nursery shelves." *Books for Keeps*

At Home with Tom and Pippo   0-7445-3721-5
Out and About with Tom and Pippo   0-7445-3720-7
£3.99 each

THREE PICTURE STORIES

Each of the titles in this series contains three classic stories of pre-school life,
first published individually as First Picture Books.

"Everyday stories of family life, any one of these humorous depictions of
the trials of an under five will be readily identified by children and adults …
buy them all if you can." *Books For Your Children*

One Day with Mum   0-7445-3722-3
A Bit of Dancing   0-7445-3723-1
A Really Great Time   0-7445-3724-X
£3.99 each

MINI MIX AND MATCH BOOKS

Originally published as Heads, Bodies and Legs these fun-packed
little novelty books each contain 729 possible combinations!

"Good value, highly imaginative, definitely to be looked out for." *Books For Your Children*

Animal Allsorts   0-7445-3705-3
Puzzle People   0-7445-3706-1
£2.99 each